CARI BEST

Bug Off!

A Story of Fireflies and Friendship

Pictures by
JENNIFER PLECAS

Farrar Straus Giroux
New York

For four of my favorite bugs:
Leo, Ivy, Max, and Jack —C.B.

For Nick! —J.P.

Farrar Straus Giroux Books for Young Readers
An imprint of Macmillan Publishing Group, LLC
175 Fifth Avenue, New York, NY 10010

Text copyright © 2019 by Cari Best
Pictures copyright © 2019 by Jennifer Plecas
All rights reserved
Color separations by Embassy Graphics
Printed in China by Hung Hing Off-set Printing Co. Ltd.,
Heshan City, Guangdong Province
Designed by Monique Sterling
First edition, 2019
1 3 5 7 9 10 8 6 4 2

mackids.com

Library of Congress Cataloging-in-Publication Data

Names: Best, Cari, author. | Plecas, Jennifer, illustrator.
Title: Bug off! / Cari Best ; pictures by Jennifer Plecas.
Description: New York : Farrar Straus Giroux, 2019. | Summary: Maude hopes
     her newfound knowledge of fireflies will win her a spot in the
     neighborhood Bug-of-the-Month Club, but Louise, the club's hard-to-please
     leader, will not let her join. | Includes a list of books and online
     resources for learning more about fireflies.
Identifiers: LCCN 2018039567 | ISBN 9780374380625 (hardcover)
Subjects: | CYAC: Clubs—Fiction. | Fireflies—Fiction. | Behavior—Fiction.
Classification: LCC PZ7.B46579 Bug 2019 | DDC [E]—dc23
LC record available at https://lccn.loc.gov/2018039567

ISBN: 9780374380625

Our books may be purchased in bulk for promotional, educational, or business use. Please
contact your local bookseller or the Macmillan Corporate and Premium Sales Department
at (800) 221-7945 ext. 5442 or by email at MacmillanSpecialMarkets@macmillan.com.

Maude had never seen a firefly until she moved from the city to the country. "They sparkle like little firecrackers," she remarked one night, "but without all the noise."

Understandably, Maude was very excited when she discovered
that one of her new neighbors, Louise, had started a Bug-of-the-Month
Club. *I can learn about fireflies and make some friends*, she thought.
But as she read the fine print, she saw that she needed to give a
speech about a bug to be invited to join.

How hard can that be? she asked herself.

With the help of several firefly books from the library, Maude painstakingly recorded and memorized some illuminating firefly facts. "Louise will love this one, and this one, and especially this one," she said.

On the night of her speech, Maude caught eleven fireflies. She gently placed them in a special lantern that had a screen on top so the fireflies could breathe.

But when she arrived at the June meeting of the Bug-of-the-Month Club, all Louise said was, "Make it snappy, Maude. We haven't got all night."

So with shaky knees, Maude began. "*Firefly* is another name for the lightning bug. Their glow comes from a light-emitting organ in their bodies. Did you know that different kinds of grown-up fireflies might flash orange or yellow or even green? They blink their lights to tell one another things like, 'I like your light,' or, 'It feels like it's going to rain.'"

"Cool!" said Amy and Victor and Ashley and Donald, applauding Maude's thoughtful selection of firefly facts. Louise, Maude noticed, was not applauding. *She must be waiting until the end of my speech,* Maude guessed.

"There are more than two thousand species of fireflies. But only some kinds flash," said Maude. "For example, fireflies in western states like California and Colorado don't."

"Too bad," said Amy and Victor.

Louise, Maude noticed, let out a long, exasperated, noisy yawn. So Maude tried harder.

"People can use fireflies to light their way in caves, through woods, and in their own bedrooms, like I do," said Maude. "But only for a day. Then I let them go. See the moist paper towel at the bottom of my firefly lantern? I keep it there in case the fireflies are thirsty." Maude held up her lantern. Eleven fireflies happily blinked on and off.

"Oh, I almost forgot: Don't let your pets eat fireflies. They taste bitter and can be poisonous," she added.

"Yikes!" said Donald and Ashley, who had dogs and cats and rabbits.

Louise, Maude noticed, was tapping her foot. "Hurry up, Maude," she said. So Maude hurried.

"A firefly's light contains an important substance that some scientists believe will enable them to cure diseases, clean up water pollution, and learn about life on other planets. That's what I want to do when I go to college: study fireflies," said Maude.

"Way to go!" said Amy and Victor and Donald and Ashley.

Louise folded her arms. "Time to wrap it up, Maude," she said.

But I have so much more to share, thought Maude. "Okay," she said politely, thinking that Louise must like short speeches.

"In conclusion," said Maude, "the firefly population is dwindling as we speak because many humans are not paying enough attention to what these little creatures need in order to survive. You are all welcome to visit my backyard tomorrow night to see what I do to keep fireflies safe."

Maude stepped back. "Thank you for your time," she told Louise and the other members of the Bug-of-the-Month Club. *I will sparkle like a firefly if Louise invites me to join her club*, she thought.

Instead Louise slowly walked over to a poster tacked to a tree. "I am not pleased," she hissed.

No one said a word.

"We obviously know something that Maude doesn't," said Louise, "and that is that the firefly—or lightning bug—belongs to the BEETLE family . . . and BEETLES ARE NOT . . . I repeat . . . ARE NOT TRUE BUGS."

She pointed at the poster.

"These are true bugs," she said,
and read the whole list.

THIS MONTH'S BUGS

AMBUSH BUG   PIRATE BUG

ASSASSIN BUG   PLANT BUG

BEDBUG   SEED BUG

BIG-EYED BUG   SOLDIER BUG

DAMSEL BUG   STINKBUG

WATER BUG

"The facts about true bugs are indisputable," said Louise.

"Everyone please take a turn."

"A bug has a head like a triangle," said Amy.

"A firefly does not," said Louise.

"A bug has a mouth like a beak," said Donald.

"A firefly does not," said Louise.

"A bug has two wings on each side—for a total of four altogether," said Ashley.

"Some fireflies also have four wings," said Louise, "but some female fireflies have no wings."

"And most importantly," said Victor, "a bug may have the word *bug* as part of its name—"

"But that doesn't necessarily make it a bug," said Ashley.

"Like a lightning bug," said Donald, "which, as Louise told us—"

"Is actually a beetle," finished Amy.

"Beetles and bugs are not the same at all," said the Bug-of-the-Month Club members in unison. "But they are both insects."

"There you have it," said Louise. "Thank you, members." And to Maude, she said, "Bye-bye, firefly. Time for you to bug off!"

Then, to make matters worse, Louise removed the top of Maude's lantern and dumped out all eleven fireflies. Not one of them flashed orange or yellow or even green as they flew away.

Maude's cheeks burned. And so did the tips of her ears.

She was mortified. *Everyone must think I'm so dumb*, Maude thought. She picked up her empty firefly lantern and walked home in the dark. *Louise. Makes. Me. So. Mad*, Maude thought. With each step, she grew even madder. *Someday, I am going to let Louise have it for being rude and nasty*, she decided.

The next night, there was a spectacular firefly show in
Maude's backyard. The neighbors noticed. So did members of
the Bug-of-the-Month Club, who had liked Maude's speech so
much that they came over to see for themselves exactly what
she was doing to protect fireflies.

Maude was surprised and happy to see them.

"It's important to create a peaceful, firefly-friendly habitat," Maude explained, "where fireflies can live and breathe and stay healthy. I keep outside lights off because fireflies like to signal to one another in the dark and may not come here if the lights are on. I found pieces of dead logs in the woods and put them under these pine trees because firefly eggs, which can glow, too, need a natural place to hatch and grow. Once they hatch into little worms or larvae, I look for snails and slugs for them to eat until they grow up to be adult fireflies. And I plant flowers because some adult fireflies like their nectar and pollen. Zinnias are my favorite flowers!"

"I want to save the firefly!" said Amy.

"So do we!" said Victor and Donald and Ashley—
and some other neighbors, too!

At the July meeting of the Bug-of-the-Month Club, Louise
wondered what had happened to all of her members . . . until
she walked around the neighborhood and saw everyone in
Maude's backyard at a Save-the-Firefly meeting.

Louise watched. She listened. "Hmm," she said to herself.
"There are things that even a bug genius like me can learn."

Maude watched. She listened. She thought, *I think it's
about time for me to let Louise have it.*

And she did.

"Welcome to the Save-the-Firefly Club, Louise," said Maude. "The more dedicated and passionate members we get, the better chance the firefly will have to make it in this often cruel world of ours."

At the August meeting of the Bug-of-the-Month Club,
Louise announced that she was changing her club's name to
the Insect-of-the-Month Club, and that Maude, whom Louise
herself had personally invited, would be a member after all.

"I should not have been so hard to please," said
Louise. "From now on, anyone can join my club. And by the
way, the firefly is now one of my favorite insects!"

Maude sparkled like a firefly.

A NOTE FROM THE AUTHOR

I am Maude and Maude is me! Not until I moved out of a big city and got a backyard of my own did I ever see a real live flashing firefly. For many years, I have done whatever I can to make sure that my favorite insect and its family and friends have a firefly-friendly environment in which to live and grow and play. I hope you will do the same for your favorite insects.

IF YOU WANT TO KNOW MORE ABOUT FIREFLIES, YOU MIGHT LIKE:

Bugs Are Insects by Anne Rockwell, illustrated by Steve Jenkins. New York: HarperCollins Publishers, 2001.

Fireflies! by Julie Brinckloe. New York: Macmillan, 1985.

Insects: A Guide to Familiar American Insects, revised and updated edition, by Herbert S. Zim, Clarence Cottam, et al. New York: St. Martin's Press, 2001.

What's That Bug? Everyday Insects and Their Really Cool Cousins by Nan Froman, illustrated by Julian Mulock. Boston: Little, Brown, 2001.

ONLINE RESOURCES

mnn.com/earth-matters/animals/stories/fireflies-12-things-you-didnt-know-about-lightning-bugs

nationalgeographic.com/animals/invertebrates/group/fireflies

nwf.org/Educational-Resources/Wildlife-Guide/Invertebrates/Fireflies

smithsonianmag.com/science-nature/14-fun-facts-about-fireflies-142999290

thoughtco.com/fascinating-facts-about-fireflies-1968117